T0193426

PORT HAVEN

REFUGE AND SANCTUARY

William Milborn

authorHOUSE®

AuthorHouse™
1663 Liberty Drive
Bloomington, IN 47403
www.authorhouse.com
Phone: 1 (800) 839-8640

Published by AuthorHouse 05/23/2019

ISBN: 978-1-7283-1296-5 (sc)
ISBN: 978-1-7283-1295-8 (e)

Introduction

(SYNOPSIS OF THE NARRATIVE)

This book is about the joseph worthy family that immigrated to this country. It tells the story of the worthy family finding their way west to the gold fields where he and his son discovered gold and became wealthy. It tells of their journey east for a more peaceful life. They find their way to the beginnings of a port called port haven refuge. Joseph and his son Joe decided to spend part of their fortune purchasing three-hundred acres where he built a sanctuary for birds on their southern fly-away.

It tells the story of how the sanctuary of many lakes was developed. You need to know that his wealth had allowed them to use their money in philanthropic ways to develop the sanctuary and invest in the many businesses surrounding the sanctuary.

They also built a fine manor where the worthy family settled. It tells of his contribution to all the needs of the port, which was a refuge for the many boats on the river which needed to stop for dry dock repairs.

He spread his wealth in contracting with farmers throughout the area to grow grain crops for all the birds flying into the many ponds and lakes on this huge sanctuary. You will see how he helped other businesses build and develop. The entertainment will be in the reading of the many interesting and unique characters that operated their businesses. This is a unique story where port haven and the bird sanctuary grew together and found they needed one another. In all this is a story of success and how one man and his family created a remarkable union between the port and the town. You will love the characters; they are as real as they could be.

I, William Worthy, am telling this story and i am the grandson and fourth generation of the worthy family.

PORT HAVEN REFUGE

List of Characters

Mr. Joseph Worthy - Founder of Port Haven Refuge

William Worthy - Founders grandson

Mr. Moses - Guns and Knives

Gloria - Eider down pillow factory

Mr. Housman - Wentsworth Tradeschool

Mrs. Booker - School principal

Ms. Phroggsbottom - Primary teacher, gardener, invented phroggsbottom tulips

Mrs. Notestrum – Music teacher (there were 100 students in the school)

Tilly - A skinny student at the trade school and took care of bookers horse

Bully Tamer – Theater major

Techat Totter - Substitute teacher – specialty discesting frogs

Mr. Tooley - Hardware store

Mr. Sawyer - Saw mill

Thelma - Fishery

Dr. Fowler - Veternarian

Smokey - Fire department

Mr. Surry - Carriage maker

Mr. Wiley Gunderson - Police chief

Mr. Wheatfield - Seed store

Mr. Cutter - Lawn and farm equipment

Mr. Elmer Voltley - Electric department

Bertha - Voltley's wife

Sally Forth - Billing department, electric company

Carla Lincoln-Jefferson - New accountant at electric company

Bessie - Carla's sister

Reverand preachly - Pastor

Reverand Wisely - New pastor

Joshua and Jeramiah - Employees of postal department

Ben Courtly - Judge

Justin - Lawyer

Bailey, warrant and finely - Law firm

Tom Speeder - Driving test

Chuck Copy - News editor

Terri Hartley - Restaurantuer

Ralph Cutler - Terri hartley's boyfriend

Lisa and Ray Shears - barbershop

Carolyn Combs - Cosmotologist

Dolly - Carolyn's friend

Mr. Honeycutt - Owner of food barn

Dr. Ted Mendmen - General practioner

Jeannette Worthy - Wife of william

Sally - The assessor

Ms. Merriam - Librarian

Elmo Voltly - Electric company

Jessie Beauregard Jefferson - Caretaker of worthy's manor and sanctuary

Tessie Jefferson – Wife of Beauregard and housekeeper of worthy's manor

Mr. Silo - Barly farmer

Mr. Oatis - Oat field farmer

Mr. Cribbs - Corn field farmer

Mr. Winnow - Wheat field farmer

Mayor - Undecided, no one seemed qualified

Mr. Innman - Inn keeper

Mr. Lacer - Shoe store

"Big George" - Security at refuge

Virgil Caine - Deputy

Mrs. Coney - Ice cream parlor

Danny - Shariff's son

Judge Judy

Sarah Courrier - Rodeo trick rider

Foo Chu - Taxi driver

Dr. Fowler - Doctor at sanctuary

Lisa - Barber's wife

Robert Townsend - Post office

Sally the assessor

"Moody Melody" - License beaureau

Sister Francis - Hospital director

Josh - High school jock

Mark summerly – Gunshop owner

Daniel Dently – Auto and repair business

Carlin Wheeler – Auto sales company

Port Haven Refuge

Joseph worthy was the creator of this Grand River port. He was a loving, caring and very giving man. He was beloved to all those that got to know him. His touch bestowed happiness and success of the institutions and businesses that he happily assisted in every way. In today's vernacular he would be considered a philanthropist.

Mr. Joseph Worthys' parents were immigrants from Ireland and Germany. They ventured far to the west in search of land. It was in a small Colorado town that he was raised by his parents.

When they passed away, joseph met an Irish girl who had come with her parents to settle. Joseph and his wife lived at his parents homestead and bore a son named joe worthy. At an early age, Joe went to work at a mill in a creek in Colorado where he found his fortune. Joe was one of the first men to discover that creek, which was a gold-filled creek. He mined that creek and he and his Irish wife became extrordinarily rich. Joseph and his son found an abundance of gold in that mill creek, and both became independently rich.

Both, on occasion, were confronted by gold thieves. The knowledge of gold in Colorado was bringing thousands of men with gold fever to the area.

The two families, joseph and his son Joe, with their wives, decided to go back east where the country was more civilized. Their trip would be by wagon, the same way they came, only this time they came with ranchers that were driving their herds back east to be sold.

Joseph and his son Joe both loved the land and decided they would use their fortune to buy it. The state offered the large land grant if they would build and promote the territory. They purchased the land around a landing and three hundred acres. This was a time that both federal and state land grants were given. The land grants would be given providing worth would spend at least three thousand dollars to build on and improve the three hundred acres and to report on the river. They were one of the first to decide to invest in the river landing and turn it into a port for river crafts of all sizes. They built a two-lane road circumnavigating the entire three hundred acre estate. They made a portion of the acreage, which contained the deep spring lake and all of its ponds, a refuge for all birds.

We had signed certified contract with the state, it would be known as the worthy estate. Joseph, for the first time since losing his wife, had a sparkle in his eyes and the will to fulfill his dream for this plan.

Joseph told his son that he would give all of his fortune to be spent on the sanctuary for birds. Their dream was singular. Until joseph died he would endow his money to the people and development of the area.

Joe and his dad built a fantastic manor that joseph declared was overspending, and could not see how they ever would have a need for such a house. The manor was built and all the carpenters and builders in that part of the country earned a good living during its two years of construction.

At this moment in time, I am inspired to reveal to y0u all the mysteries and wonderments of this little town called port haven (and bird refuge), U.S.A. Someday I will be an owner of this three-hundered acre "shang-gra-la" for ducks and geese. Many ponds on the three-hundred acres lured ducks and geese on their fly-away to rest there before going south.

Many stayed to make it their home. That is why there are so many varfieties of our feathered friends. Many of these gorgeous birds chose the little ponds as their permanent residence for the fish as well as the grain. I, Mr. William worthy, will be the fortunate owner of this grand place, and I will happily be the primary reason for the increased number of ducks and geese that come here on their regular fly-away south.

I am happy to recall, that as a young lad visiting these ponds, I would lay back and rest and experience the view of the grassy flora and fauna and listen to the croaking of the frogs that raised their voices at my presence. I recall that when I was asleep by one of these ponds, that when I awoke, I saw ducks looking into my face. I can't imagine what those ducks may have thought as they suddenly flew away quacking when I opened my eyes. I think that those ducks may have communicated, somehow, with all the thousands of other winged beauties, that I was okay, and not to be feared. Now I must reveal what the presence of these thousands of feathered friends on these ponds have done for the quakers in this township.

At first, I felt that because of the number of birds, that I should feed them. But that would be more than I could afford. So, I had an inspiration to let the world know that this was a grand vacationing experience.

It worked, and the tourists came here by the hundreds every year. They come frequently to visit port haven. Many of the town folks who benefit from this also helped build the paths to and around the ponds. The tourists visit the three-hundred acres covered with beautiful trees and flowers everywhere. The primary reason of anticipation of the visitors was to witness a myriad of our feathered friends. The ducks would very often dive into the water for food, and they would use the paths to follow the visitors and get morsels of food now and then. The ducks would be friendlier if they felt that they were safe.

There were so many varieties of ducks and geese. I bought thousands of "small fries" from the local fisheries and introduced them to the ponds.

The quacking and honking was musical but loud, as they dove in to enjoy a taste of seafood. On top of this, i asked my farmer friends if they could grow assorted grains all around my three-hundred acres so my duck friends could forage the fields at their leisure and complete their diet.

I know that you are wondering, how would I pay for this? How else but by imposing a small admission price that the guests would pay to stroll the paths around the ponds and feed the ducks. Many of the ducks and geese, by their own inclination, would eat directly from the hands of the tourists. My, how exciting! (for little kids and big ones too). Soon, these admission funds grew to an extraordinary amount of money. Now I could afford to pay the farmers and the fisheries for their efforts.

I had contacted Thelma and offered to pay her to provide a regular delivery of "small fry" to the many ponds on the three-hundred acres. My funds had grown so I gave her a bonus to continue to deliver the fish. It was critical to feed our ducks and geese friends. She would say "thank you", and gived me a hug and kiss and say, "now I can get my children through school."

I wanted the refuge to be financially capable of continuing its existence without depending on contributions, including myself. The operation would now find it self-reliant because I had established an admission charge. I still had the farmers I contracted to grow the grain for my ducks. They would be paid for their work through the dmission charges.

I contracted one of the town's original residents, Gloria. She had lost her husband and was maintaining a livelihood as a seamstress. I offered her, what I thought to be, a brilliant opportunity to make pillows. I set her up in business and let her pick her own staff. Her new business made pillows from the down and feathers that she would be provided to her for a pillow factory. I am sad to say that even the ducks and geese have their day. Even ducks pass away.

I had the refuge caretaker, Jessie, collect the many birds on the ponds that had gone to duck and goose heaven and bring them to my sanctuary. There was an ample number that would not live. Hunting birds outside of our refuge caused many to receive fatal injuries which caused them to fly into the lake and ponds. I brought all of those ducks and geese back to my sanctuary – back to my home.

There were two sections of the sanctuary. Those birds that were curable, my duck doctor – Dr. Fowler – would remove the shot and nurse them until they could fly. They would be treated by the veterinarian, and many of the birds decided to stay. In the other part of our sanctuary there were treatment areas. We were disappointed that even with our help they died and went to duck and goose heaven. Our haven was their portal to heaven.

Those that did not make it were sent to Gloria's pillow factory where I had built a processing building. This is where the ducks and geese would be processed for their down and feathers. Gloria's pillows were gorgeous and so soft. She called them "her pillows". She marketed them throughout the Quakers land. The township now had a slogan. It was "Quaker's quackers – from port haven!" It was sewn into every pillow lining.

Thelma's fisheries was also building boat slips for lease and sending out her own fishing boats to bring an assortment of fresh fish to sell in her new fish market. I was so happy that the farmers, who grew the grain, Thelma's fishery, and Gloria's business making "her pillows" were flourishing.

I hope everyone at some point in this chronology has a new appreciation of people that have ambition, and people who create things, and the power of creating jobs. The real heroes of this story are the gorgeous feathered friends and their continuous quacking and honking.

To every happy story there is always a hazardous element that arises. Have you guessed what? All around my three-hundred acre refuge there is now being built processing plants for ducks and geese that have been killed by commercial and business hunters. The ducks and geese are processed for their feathers and down.

Thank god that the regular meat markets do not accept wild geese and ducks to be sold. From the three-hundred acres, the birds are flying out to the grain fields and the birds are being shot from the sky by hunters from their blinds.

I have never known how to stop the killing of the ducks and geese. It is said that the entire three-hundred acres are bordered by duck and goose blinds. Hunters purchase licenses from the state which provides them with the authority to shoot ducks and geese from blinds located outside the refuge. The outside processing plants would sell to Gloria's pillow factory all the down and feathers she needed. That to me is the only good I could see.

Many of the thousands of ducks and geese on the three-hundred acres of ponds will continue the flight to the south or stay here and live.

Collection Booths

I want to tell you more about the six booths used for collections surrounding port haven's duck sanctuary. A change was made in the earlier cash receipt proceeds and now the collection booths receive the entrance fees for which receipts are given and copies kept. They are placed ion the iron box and locked at sunset. Big George, our one and only security man, collected the receipts and cash from each booth. He is prepared to protect these important receipts and cash. He delivers them straight to the manor where he puts them through a special receiving slot to the left of the manor doorway. Tessie takes charge of them from there. The booths have an extended private rest room for their use only. The booths have sides that could be lowered in good weather and closed in bad weather. They are closed at the end of each shift at dusk. The senior booth attendants have more once called big George, our security officer, to remove unwelcome cars and people who were not authorized to be in the parking area and he entered the refuge to remove violators that broke the rules, as I explained earlier. The size of Big George was all he needed to handle most of the incidents.

The parking area that was so beautiful is laden with trees and flowers. It is so pretty that there is a temptation for the passers by to use the park for a while, also the high school students. I have begun to think that this place is a great hangout area. Signs at the park's entrance say only for the guests visiting the refuge. Thank goodness for Big George. Who is Big George? He is Wiley Gunderson's big brother who is a famous ex-wrestler and is retired and living in our town. His wages were meager. He received satisfaction from the power he weiled and the police car he drove. He was priceless. I for one think that big George is a real asset to our town.

Besides the refuge for the birds, port haven refuge is equally famous for its contribution to all the captains that float their craft on the river. Our town's port, over this time period, has seen many crippled vessels limping into this port. Some could have easily sunk to the bottom of the river. The captains of those boats call this port heaven instead of port haven. Heaven knows what could have happened to those captains and their crews had it not been for this port. Many of the crafts can be seen in dry dock where gapes in their bows and undersides were being repaired. Again, it was the endowment of Joe Worthy and his contribution to our port authority that the miracle of this port continues to thrive. The name port heaven seems to be contagious. There are many in our town that are calling it that.

One company is building a new boat in one of the large dry docks. It will be the biggest transport and fishing boat on our river. The boat has already been named "gratitude" because one of the captains (captain rivers), was saved by one of the several rescue boats that are manned by the coast guard. The coast guard rescue craft are added by the government as they saw port haven (heaven) grow as it has.

Interestingly, to conserve the way of the old salts, a swinging door tavern was built on the river. For the captain and his crews it was really the only place to go for food, brew and entertainment.

There was a hint of the old pirate days as they referred to the waitress as a wench, but it was all in good spirits. The names of the drinks would remind you of the pirate days in jest: such as grog, whaler rum, ale, and meade. They were served there. Eventually, many of our townspeople found their way there for the adventure of the place.

The bar was adorned with many treasure maps to add mystique for the many men and women that enjoyed the port. They enjoyed the pub all day and evenings too. One of the several barkeepers was called hook and he brought out his wooden leg and hook and placed them for all to see in front of the bottled whisky and rum.

It was true that there were skirmishes of the boats' crew that Gunderson, our sheriff, and his deputy had to break up. In fact, fines were given. Our town council decided there would be a third deputy hired to patrol the port area and break up bad situations before they got too difficult.

The requirement for the deputy they hired was that he must look like an ex-wrestler, tall, and rough looking. It was felt that intimidation by a patrolman would carry a lot of weight when he visited troubled areas, and it did.

I do not think grandpa Joe Worty had any idea that port haven (heaven) would grow as it had. Its was reputation is known all up and down the river. Our town's council and port authority agreed that there should be a second more dignified "booze palace" for those that wished to dine and drink in peace and quiet on the water front of our port haven refuge.

We are not through with describing the township of port haven. First we have an abundance of wonderful children that attend our Quaker church and many other churches and listen to the religious sermons. The Quaker pastor had the unusual name of reverand preachly. Reverand Preachly spent most of the time beating and pounding his fist on the dias and spoke of devils and damnation to all that were there, instead of preaching the gospel. The children were wide-eyed and anxious as well as their parents and the rest of the congregation for the services to be over.

I, too, was anxious for the last amens, because preachly had nearly convinced me that I was going to hell. I considered seeking another church or outlet to god. I swiftly made my exit into a bright sunshining spring day. I hopped aboard my scooter and sped off to my large beautiful manor on the hill. As I made my way I could see that one of the parking lots was already filling up with tourists. There were so many. They were coming from all directions. I had built six parking areas surrounding my three-hundred acres of ponds. I had the acreage protected by tall wooden fencing to make it seem more natural to the environment. There were six entrances through those fences to the parking areas. I kept those parking areas like a golf course green. There was grass instead of pavement or tar. I kept in mind that the ducks and geese walked there too. From the parking area the guests could choose to meander around the many ponds.

The tourists would pay a small admission price to enter the refuge. I paid mine as well. Teenagers from the schools were interviewed and hired and i had them collect these donations at the gates entrances. There bonuses depended on attendance and attention to their assignments.

Over each parking gate there was a specially mounted sign that said: port haven refuge and showed a picture of flying ducks and geese. There were other attractive signs a well that said, "no honking of your car horns – let the geese do it!" The gatekeepers were instructed to tell the guests that there would be no yelling, running, or chasing the ducks and geese, or trying to catch them. No food and beverages were allowed on the refuge except for the birds grains, which could be bought at the entrance gates. The tourists could have their food and beverages in the parking area where tables were provided.

The same information was also printed in a pamphlet. The pamphlet would contain the names of all the various ducks and geese that were in the refuge. The notice said that the gatekeeper would also call security on anyone who was violating the rules. "please treat them as if they were your houseguests or as if you were going to visit someone. You are the guests of the geese!"

There were booths for the gatekeepers to use while collecting from the visitors. Each covered booth had sides that could be raised in case of bad weather and at closing time. Each booth had a counter, a lock box for cash, and bags of food for the ducks and geese that the guests could purchase. The guests could also buy t-shirts with a flying duck and goose embossed on them. A comfortable seat was present and an electric fan as well as a telephone. The booth was wired for electricity to provide a large extended light over the entrance of the parking area. There were two students hired for each booth to cover the hours from dawn until dusk. At dusk the booth and parking area would be secured for the night. The booth attendent, be it boy or girl, would put the cash and receipts into a locked bag and they would give the bag to a security agent who would pick up the locked bag and receipts at closing. The guard would go to the worthy's manor gate. The safe had an alarm system and the area was well lighted. William worthy's accountant would open the safe with a key and place the money in Mr. Worthy's account. The receipts were then sent to Tessie murphy, or to me. So much for receiving and controlling the funds from port haven refuge.

A teenage representative at each gate explained to all visiting guests that the donations were for the upkeep of the park, the paths, the ducks and geese, and the fish.

Each parking areas was surrounded by wild flowers and some special perrenials were planted. I must tell you that this was a pleasurable project that I wanted to do around my acreage. I called it my hobby! All the planting brought a number of colorful birds to the area. What better way to spend some of the profits I had realized from the visitors and vacationers. With all of the advertizements I have had through T.V. And radio, we were not without hundreds of visitors each year. Now we were on the map! It was not uncommon to find the six parking areas filled with parked cars. I mentioned the state awarded proiveleges for hunters, but I had not mentioned that the several processing plants that the hunters took their quarry to, sold their down and feathers to "Gloria's pillow factory" at a low price. This allowed her to maintain an inventory of down and feathers that would insure the continuous production of "her haven pillows". Gloria was now contracting with retail stores throughout the state and even out-of-state to purchase "her haven pillows". Gloria and I had a contract. I received a generous percentage of the profits and maintained our duck and goose haven. All of the business owners and other citizens surrounding Mr. Worthy's three-hundred acres of ponds were grateful to me for my efforts and vision. All of the businesses, in one way or another, were all connected to the acreage in port haven and its activities.

The businesses grew around his three-hundred acres like a halo around the moon. It really wasn't a township or a city. We called our town port haven refuge, but it really was a wonderland. We now had streets and lighting that was installed with the property and real estate taxes. It is heartwarming to see port haven grow. I also thought of all my friends that were barely making it in their little businesses and were now making more profit than they ever had before. Our town was meeting the needs of the many hundreds of guests and visitors that were passing through on their vacation trips. Many vacationers wanted to live here and raise their children in our splendid port haven refuge. It was a definite stopping point for many vacationers on their vacation agenda before going to their destinations.

There was a large tributary or river passing close to my acreage that brought so many ducks and geese that it caused many of the ducks and geese to use it on their fly-away to the south. The balance of my three-hundred acres had to do with state and county roads going hither and yon. We have major highways going across the river. I provided Thelma finances for her fisheries, boat slips and a new fish market on that river. We agreed that she would in turn give me "small fries" to stock my ponds through her business at a low price based on usage. She would also deliver them to the ponds. I tell you now, I think of that fish market and the most robust fish monger I had ever seen from which I bought my fish.

Most of the businesses came from the eastern side of the river. Most all of the other customers came from the western side of the river. The major highway along the river and major highway on the other side of the river offered a myriad of ways to get to this sanctuary of mine.

As you know, I am blessed with my ponds. They are more suitable for ducks than geese. Even though this is on a goose fly-away, most of the geese look the area over and continue on to the larger lakes such as Swan Lake in Missouri. We do have many flocks of geese that fly in and over the larger ponds on the north. They have a nice rest and some food and then lift off to continue their fly-away south. Hunters take advantage of these beautiful creatures as they fly over the perimeter of port haven refuge. How sad! Geese are more skittish, and a lot of activity, cars and people can scare them off. That is another reason why they don't stay long and the only down side to having so many vacationers. The new flocks of ducks that come here have a personality or demeanor that would cause them to be less wild and more comfortable in their surroundings and soon many could be fed by hand. It is sad, I must report, that for every goose that is downed by a hunter's bullet, their mates will live alone, for they only have one mate in their lives.

Before I continue this expose, you may wish to know something about me, will worthy. At the age of twenty-four, most folks might wonder why I am still single. I wonder too. Most people would also say i look to be of a much younger age. I need to keep myself looking as young as I can look, for I am still seeking a lady who would show love for me and also have marriage in mind. Do I seek the lady or does the lady seek me?

I frankly don't know how to catch a catch. Maybe one of my readers might have an interest in briefing me in this or come see me. I am wating for someone to find me, or I must find someone. I'm still in my prime. Anyway, I'm six feet two inches tall, I have eyes of blue and still slim at the waist. I have narrow hips and strong legs. The paths that I walk at the duck haven refuge have given me plenty of exercise to keep my belly flat and my legs strong. I have rather long reddish hair, a little beyond the nape of my neck and hair is somewhat curly. I speak with a German accent due to being raised by my German grandfather, Joe.

I lost my parents when I was in college. Life would have been oh so lonely had it not been for my great grandfather, joseph worthy, and his three-hundred acre refuge.

I was holding his head when he closed his eyes the day he died. Only those that have lost a loved one can know that feeling that overwhelms you. I have said earlier that my great grandfather left me this wonderous estate with its beautiful ponds and a wish that I would continue with his dream of this sanctuary.

As we say, I remember that day as if it were yesterday. Many of great grandfather's special friends and acquaintances and kin were quietly standing around the bed. No one was crying, weeping or carrying on. It was not the nature or custom of the Irish and German to do more than silently mourn the passing of a loved one. Great grandfather had a caretaker and a housekeeper for many years. Her name was tessie murphy. She stood by his bedside, holding his hand and she whispered in his ear. Tessie came to me and led me back to great grandfather. She placed my hand in his. He firmly gripped my hand, his eyes search mine for the longest time. I felt his hand relax and saw his eyes close. He muttered, "Take care of our feathered friends". This too was in the will. I heard no breathing. Joseph worthy went away. I would never say die because he is so much alive in my memory that I can still feel his presence in and around the grounds.

Later, after the funeral rituals were over and everyone went home, I sat at his graveside and looked up at the splendid monument marking of his last resting place. I was overcome when I saw inscribed on his monument "Joseph and all of my feathered friends". Below the inscription was a large beautifully embossed duck flying skyward as if it were heaven bound. He left his long time housekeeper and his caretaker, Mr. Paul, the right to live in the estate manor for as long as they live.

It was a cool morning when I stepped onto the porch of the manor. There was a low misty fog hanging over the pond where the ducks were paddling in circles. I noticed that grandpa Joe was stationed in his old rocker, as he was early each morning, staring at the pond and ducks that he loved so well. Grandpa Joe whispered "will, please take care of my family and my birds." When you throw my ashes in the air over Spring Lake remember the ashes are not me. My spirit and soul will still be around and my spirit will still be sound. I put my hand on his shoulder. I received no response. I bent over and looked into his yees. They were glazed over and partly closed. I lowered myself onto my knees and took his hand in mine. I recall saying "oh no…oh no…oh no…" I know that I cried, whimpered and shrieked. I had lost my second father. It was then tht Tessie Murphy opened the manor door and said "you folks com on in now". Its chilly and its breakfast time.

When she saw that I was kneeling in front of grandpa, she started shrieking and squalling and cried, "no…no…no…". She repeated many times "no…no…no…". She ran to his other side and grabbed him loosely around the neck and started to whimper and cry. I stood while she mourned and this scene would be imbedded in my mind forever. Tessies' husband wondered where we were as he stepped onto the porch. He came to me and said, "I don't cry, I just hurt." He put his hand on his wife's head and said, "we'll be okay". He looked at me and said "will, you are the man of the manor now, we will need you".

He was the nucleous of every good event concerning port haven refuge. I was in mourning again. I, too, would cry again for I have lost both my great grandfather and my grandfather.

I lived in the manor after my parents died just after my college graduation. That is another story which I will not tell. I will say dad died in the war and mom of a broken heart.

The manor housekeeper, Tessie, had always taken care of me after my parents died and the will directed her to do so for the balance of my days. She was an excellent cook. It was later confirmed that I had full authority over the entire estate.

After leaving grandfathers graveside it came to me like a bolt of lightning that the estate would be "port haven refuge" with an embossed picture of a duck and a goose on every sign.

Grandpa Joe would be so pleased to see that four generations of our town are living in such harmony. Our seniors are thinking of the good old days and believe our town is suffering from growing pains. They feel so happy that our town still has a livery stable, and saddle and harness shop. It also has a business that makes carriages, buckboards, buggies, and surries. They were pleased to see some corrals with horses, and the blacksmith, Mr. Moses, making horseshoes and parts for farm equipment. They noted that their feed and seed store, run by Mr. Wheatfield, was doing a grand business. The farmers growing the crops, Mr. Silo, Mr. Oats, Mr. Cribbs and Mr. Winnow were certainly needed for their services. I am going to say that the farmers could only afford, and still were using, horses. They needed all of the services including the veteranarian, Dr. Fowler. He tended to the farm animals, and cats and dogs, etc.

The older folks were happy to see that the old town ways were still in use. The businesses were elated to see an improved usage for their wares.

Tessie

Readers, it is time I let you know that Tessie Jefferson was not only my grandpa's friend, housekeeper, and caretaker, she was an African-American. I loveds her and she took good care of me.

Two cololred house maids would see to my every need. Grandpa's best friend Jessie Beauregard Jefferson, went to college and joined the service to fight in Korea.

Prior to his going off to war, he married a light-skinned African-American girl. Grandpa Joe Worthy, in respect for his friend, gave Mrs. Jefferson a job as a maid and housekeeper. The will, as mentioned earlier, stated that Tessie could live in the manor for the rest of her life. Joe called Mrs. Jefferson by her first name, Tessie. He got to know her very well. In fact, Joe felt a real fondness for Tessie and made her his caretaker and housekeeper!

Mr. Innman's Port Haven Refuge Travel Lodge

Port haven refuge was printed in a semi-circle over a semi-circle rainbow on a sign. We first see a well-lighted parking area in front of the inn. On the road leading to the inn, each of the eight parking spaces were marked "special parking – two dollars", so a customer could park there or to the side of the building or further away. The idea was that spots would be preferred for the older guests, or for bad weather. It worked. There was a yellow brick walk used for the entrance way that was open to a lobby where the ceiling was covered with paintings of blue fluffy clouds.

We are now face to face with the multi-talented innkeeper. Mr. INNMAN was not only the owner, but the desk clerk, bell-hop, repair man and accountant. Frugal would be his middle name. What he lacked in customers he more than made up for in low operation costs.

Mr. Innman would wear formal clothing with a black toupee covering his baldness. It was obvious by the gray hair of his sideburns which contrasted with his toupee. He was a tall man with large ears and smiling eyes. He mostly looked as solemn an undertaker. He would flash and ear-to-ear toothy smile, as a guest approached his counter.

His verbal greeting was far too loquacious to even try to repeat. The words spewed from his mouth. Compliments to the customers as Mr. Innman accepted the credit card or cash. When he hit the Bellon the desk it sounded more like the bell at a boxing match. It rang loud and echoed through the room. Then he would say, "Would you like my son, the bell captain, to take your luggage to your room?" When his son was not available, he would offer his own services.

His son was required to share fifty percent of his tips and pay for his own uniforms. His frugalness included his wife, mother and sister! They were the room housekeepers and he would pay them a small pittance for their services.

He had strict rules about who could stay at his inn. No smoking—no alcohol. He could smell the substances with his powerful nose. He had a nose like a bloodhound. He could see if a young woman was properly dressed and if she was applying for a room alone. Ladies of the evening were not accepted. Loud boisterous men were a no-no as well. Those that did stay were classier than at the other establishments. Mr. Innman was highly respected because of his business ethics.

Though staying at the inn seemed to be reasonable, the little charges would quickly add up. Added to the cost of the room was a sur charge for use of the maids. This would be a minimum of two dollars for maid service and cleaning.

To ensure that his housekeepers (his family), kept up with his cleaning standards, they were to keep the bathrooms so clean that a surgeon could use if for an operation. The housekeepers notified Mr. Innman if any of the shampoo, toothpaste or other incidentals were missing after the guests left, so Mr. Innman could apply a charge for that item to the bill.

The amenities, such as shampoo, would be refilled and put back as new. All televisions were available after one would place a dollar into the greedy T.V. Slot. Additionally, tissue and toilet paper were available from housekeepers for a small charge. There was also a charge for extra towels.

The recalcitrant potential guests would be told to leave and be informed that any problem would be dealt with by the local police.

Reverand Wisely

The other church of port haven was established as a result of the businesses. The pillow factory, fishery, and Mr. Worthy donated money to procure land to build the church.

Their problem was that they needed someone to lead this second church. Stan wisely was a lowly farm worker and unhappy with his wages so he went to church. He suddenly noted that at the end of the service when the church plates were passed, money would pile on the plates. He informed the pastor that he had a calling and said "I want to be a reverand."

He still needed a license so he went to school to become a reverand. This schooling took the whole of two years. Now he's back to present the gospel. He could go anywhere. He was a natural leader of the church of port haven refuge. Ne never preached hell and damnation, but only suggested the possibility there of.

The church was called the "church of faith" and its motto was "the fruits of your labor will be increased if you give wisely". Give thanks to reverand wisely.

Mr. Tooley – Hardware Store Owner

Mr. Tooley was a charming man of sixty and proud. He had a smile that was from ear to ear. He had a broad heavy face, and he was smooth shaven. He felt he was really debonair to the ladies of his era. He would try to be flirtatious and wink at a lady but of his eyes would shut. It didn't matter that he had a short neck. He also had a very large round waist.

God, how he loved his hardware store. There wasn't one piece of hardware that he didn't know about. He was the text book of tools. He was the dictionary of nuts, bolts, and nails. It would drive Mr. Tooley crazy if he received an item from a manufacturer and didn't know what it was or how it worked. He was ashamed to ask. He would call the manufacturer or drive to the place if it was close, so he could add it to his repertoire of hardware knowledge. How proud he was to expound on any item that a customer came to buy even when the customer didn't care to hear about it.

Police Department

Mr. Gunderson has the only one-man police department in the world, and he had the fastest car in town. He keeps it like new and he would drive along and could be seen showing his magnificent car as he drove to and from the area businesses. There was never a question that it was a police car. He had a big siren and lights on top. It had a special horn which on occasion he used to shout out to business people and say "i will protect you!" He would make his existence known. Mr. Gunderson had a small place in his office which he called a jail. It had bars and it would hold at least two captured criminals or town drunks. There was never a man so proud of his position and p0wer as Mr. Gunderson. He was a well uniformed police officer with his shiny badge, shoes and car. Mr. Gunderson had his wages distributed by our town board and they surely needed to be raised. However, instead of wages he found himself receiving free meals and the café, free drinks at the pub, and free services at about everywhere in town, including the doughnut shop.

I liked Mr. Gunderson and so did anyone at my port haven refuge. Anyone could call him regularly and let him know how things were going or if they needed help. It was a relief for me to know they had someone dependable like Mr. Gunderson to contact.

At every opportunity he loved to set off his siren. If you crossed the street wrong, miss-park, went over fifteen miles per hour on main street. He set off a siren to let people know that he was on duty. When the tourists came through he would supplement the cash needed for the police department and give them a ticket.

He finally caught a serious criminal who had just made off with a six-pack of beer from a convenience store. He caught the criminal red-handed. There was no blazing fire. It was just his martial arts skills that kept the situation from escalating. Wiley Gunderson was so proud that when the eighteen year old that threatened the shop keeper with his twenty-two caliber pistol and was put behind bars, the townspeople gave him a fifty cent an hour raise. They now have given him permission to put two bullets in his pearl handled revolver. You see no guns of any kind are allowed in port haven refuge.

Even though the department was creating a deficit in the city's coffers, the board still managed to find revenue from Wiley Gunderson's police work. This included parking meters, catching more tourists that were speeding and miss-parking, running stop signs, or who had lacked a proper driver's license or insurance. Now with these possibilities and the number of tourists passing through, Mr. Gunderson would need a deputy. The deputy was a good-looking young man who wore a uniform well and spoke well. Wiley Gunderson would teach him the art of using a pistol and the things for which a ticket would be given. Our deputy's name was Virgil Caine. He could spot violators really very well. The department's revenue doubled!

One day Shariff Gunderson received a 911 call from the clothing store. A shop lifter had just taken a stack of pants and shirts and left with them. Without asking anything more Wiley told his deputy, Virgil Caine, to handle the case. Virgil jumped into that shiny police car and sped off with his siren blaring. Within minutes he arrived at the scene of the crime. Virgil, with side-arm in hand, charged into the store and said "which way did he go?" And the clerk said, "I don't know, he just left!" Virgil asked "who was it?" Everyone knew that it was Danny, our star basketball player and the police chief's son. Everyone in the store was stunned and started chattering. Virgil Caine said "my bosses boy? I can't arrest him!" He said he would just have to tell Wiley what had happened.

You have got to know, Wiley loved his son and was devastated but nevertheless, he knew the citizens were watching as their Mr. Gunderson climbed aboard his police car and went to his own house and arrested his own son – Danny – his Danny! All Danny could say was "why?... why?...why?

I don't know what deputy Caine said when Wiley arrested his own son Danny. Danny was brought back to the station and jailed like a serious criminal. This is shoplifting. This could be a long story but i will shorten it by saying that when the judge heard that Danny shoplifted the clothes and gave them to his high school best friend who was so poor that he only had the clothes he wore to go to school that day.

When judge Judy heard the details she said that nevertheless she had to punish Danny. It was decided he would have to provide community service by collecting refuse from the roadside and walkways throughout the city for the balance of the year. "What a break Danny got!" I thought. Virgil Caine, the deputy, thought the judge had a big heart. Dannys' daddy said, "not enough" and told danny that he would have to attend the states law school. Danny knew that his dad would go into debt providing his tuition. Danny cried. I liked Danny and his daddy Wiley, too, so much so that I drove Danny to the law school where we visited the dean of law and told him the story. We asked him if we could give Danny a break on tuition and the dorm too. The dean starred at me and said "who are you?" I replied, "I'm William worthy!" The dean said "you would be Joe Worthys' grandson?" I said "yes". The dean said "finally i have the chance to pay back. You know your grandfather has twice given an endowment to our law school. Funds that we needed. Danny Gunderson, I am going to give you free tuition to our law school, free dorm and free cafeteria privileges during your education at the school. I will require that you will become an assistant and apprentice to our new law firm. Though you may be tempted, do not violate our rules or be tempted by the many opportunities you will have to break the rules. If you do this opportunity will be withdrawn". As we left I said, "Danny this would have cost you thousands of dollars. How luck are you!". I said to myself, "grandpa how many good friends and good deeds have you accomplished along the way?"

Our townsfolk took on a new attitude about chief Wiley Gunderson and his son Danny. Life was fine again. Wiley was happy again and I certainly was.

However, the judge ordered the merchandise to be returned to the store. I said "judge will you allow me to purchase these clothes and let Danny's friend keep them?" The judge said "absolutely".

After Danny's friend knew that he could keep the clothes and that I had paid for them, he stated "I will help your refuge groundskeeper now and rake leaves the rest of the year. Please let me thank you!" I accepted the offer. Now I understand why this was Danny's best friend. P.s.: "he was one of the best dressed kids in school."

The anniversary date of port haven refuge is that date on which joseph worthy bought the three-hundred acres near the river. This small journal that I am writing is used in grade school and high school history classes. It is required testing. Ot is the best and only way all the young people coming of age will know how our town came to be and understand how it is that we have selected the anniversary date of our town.

It is my honor, now and then, to present a parade in honor of those who have made our town possible. This year has passed and I have rented and bought several floats, large and small, so each business on main street and the river port can decorate their own float where they can advertise their business, sing, dance, or play their music – whatever they come up with.

Business folks know that my expectations for them to participate is very high. Sometimes I have to remind the businesses on the port and in the town that they have all been financed by joseph worthy, joe worthy, and myself, William Worthy.

I wasn't sure if the afore mentioned businesses and agencies in this book would have the imagination to create a fun and interesting float. I was very surprised at what they created by themselves or with help. They were interesting and creative floats. I'm sure some must have paid someone to help with the business themes for their floats.

I noticed the businesses that realized more profits created the bigger and better floats. Not only did the businesses present the themes of their floats, but they rode the float, waving to the crowds. There were some agencies -- sheriff, F.B.I., post office, library, that rented a fancy car, wagon or automobile for the parade. I rented a carriage and led the parade, at the request of the city council, with the high school band following just behind me and the floats.

We had a number of cheerleaders that followed the high school band on the main street. To describe, you can just imagine each of the businesses and how they presented their floats. They used everything from wagons to tractors. The businesses had their families on the floats. They were waving, cheering, singing or waving a flag. I can't recall how may vehicles and people there were at the parade. The crowd cheered and showed their appreciation.

After my carriage and the band, the barber, Mr. Shears, and his wife rode a small float with a barber pole erected in the middle of his float. He played his accordian and sang along with his wife and a Bulgargian buddy. That will give you an inkling of what was seen. It took ten minutes for the complete parade from beginning to end to complete its course.

Unlike other parades the floats would end up at our town's fairgrounds. The fairgrounds were built several years ago to accommodate small carnivals and circuses that came through. It also served as a place where the city could show and sell the city farmers' produce and cattle. The bbq guys could enter a contest. They would be judged by a panel of judges and receive trophies. For producing this years best bbq, there generally six participants. There was one award for presentation, one for taste, and one for tenderness. They bbq'd any time of meat they chose.

There were a number of booths for individuals offering quilts for sale. Other booths presented and sold hand made jewelry and home canning. There were prizes to be won and awarded to another set of participants. There were booths for bakery presentations. There were samples offered to everyone passsing the fair booth.

There was a large gazaebo in the middle of the fairground. In the evening they would offer music played by an assortment of musical instruments and the high school orchestra.

The people attending would dance to ballroom, modern dance and slow dancing. Lighting was provided by courtesy of the electric company. Well, I got off the subject when I mentioned the fairgrounds. I was saying that our parade ended at the fairgrounds where a building supply company put up pre-made sturdy fences.

This was rodeo time. Everyone in the parade dispersed and went home.

The best place around the rodeo to take it all in was the arena. Our rodeo did not have an automatic animal shoot from which the animals were released. We had men for eight unbroken horses that several of the farmers brought in for the young men of the town to ride for "guts and glory". We had two clocksmen to measure the times our adventuresome riders could stay on an unbroken horse. The best times were recorded for each rider. The longest times recorded by the riders were saved and the riders would have a contest to play off for the best times. The case awards for first, second, and third place, were given to the best young riders of our town.

Normally the rodeo had no bulls to ride. Well, we have one old lazy bull and he was ridden by a clown – our Sherrif Gunderson. What a comic relief that was.

The arena was now cleared and a number of grade school children with their parents blessing, volunteered to chase down young wild greased pigs. Any kid that could catch and hold one of the pigs for a few seconds would win a small monetary award. I wish you could have seen the number of kids trying to chase and hold onto those greased pigs!

After that there was a sheep riding contest for kids from fifth through eighth grades. The kids, with parents' permission, would try to ride them. The two or three that managed to stay on the sheep for a few seconds would win according to the best three times.

The final event of the rodeo was a tall skinny lady named Sarah Courrier. She knew that she had the shortest horse in town. She had wagons with hay bales for seats which she would rent to groups for hay wagon rides in the fall. She rented riding horses for a fee and would tell folks how to ride. She received pay for riding lessons.

Sarah Courrier cared for and kept eight well-mannered riding horses. She trained them so they would not be easily spooked by anything. She trained the horses to be walking horses; unlike many horses where the ride would be a bumpy one.

The gate to the arena was opened and in she came, dressed as a cowgirl. She had a small saddle but she did horse riding tricks that marveled us all. She rode standing on her hands, side-saddle, backward, and standing on the haunches of her pony as it raced around the arena. She, at one point, while standing on the horses haunches, twirled a lasso that she had stashed on the saddle. She rode blindfolded. The more the folks applauded the more tricks she performed. When the horse was exhausted the rodeo announcer said "that's all folks".

Most folks gathered up their picnic baskets and headed to the park to enjoy more music, chat and tell stories. You can see why this rodeo event was something the townspeople had looked forward to and has become an annual event.

Food Barn

Our food barn dispensed food and meats and other items like no other I have known. In the backlot of the store there was a hugh enclosure. It was a place for the cows and pigs. The townspeople called the store the food barn. It was famous for its fresh meats, featuring beef, pork and chicken.

The cows were purchased by the owners who had a large slaughter house. From there the meat was iced and brought directly to the food barn manager, Ray Honeycutt. There was a separate area where the pigs were fed and butchered. This was all done on an "as needed" basis.

Any overkill was not sent to the food barn but was reproccessed and fed to the pigs. Any overkill on hogs was packed up and sent to a grease rendering company. Chickens were purchased from several farmers if they could prove they were not caged chickens. The food barn would also buy their eggs as long as they were from uncaged chickens.

The food barn purchaser would contact several farmers in the area that had chickens for sale. He would base his purchases on current sales and inventory. All chickens were fresh as well as other meats. The same was true at augustus turkey farm two miles away.

The food barn owned and operated a smokehouse to provide smoked items based on inventory and sales, on one condition, that the meat manager bought the hogs directly from the food barn butchery.

This all required an immense government check from the food and drug officials. The meat would be checked to ensure all of the meat was fresh. He hired two experts from the agricultural school to monitor the rules and regulations for freshness of beef, pork, chicken and eggs.

The food barn was strict at serving noting but fresh food and none of it was given to charity. After two days on the shelf all products would go the pig lot to be ground up and fed to the hogs and added to their grains or their slop.

Ray Honeycutt required three butchers who processed all cuts of meat to order. Some standard cuts were displayed in film wrap and buried in ice around the counter for those customers who were in a hurry. The butch encouraged every customer to allow a butcher to cut the meat for quantity and size. Cut to order meat could be bought for slightly less, where there would be no worry if the meat left on the shelf was wasted or for the cost of the wrapping.

Mr. Honeycutt could barely keep up with the demand of our townspeople. In fact, every customer had to show that he was a resident or a river port resident. All others were denied. A card was required and again you must be a resident of good standing and have good credit. That is the way it is for our famous meat and food barn, and well known for it throughout the area.

Another young entrepreneur named Terri Hartly, who was a food service management graduate from the state college, was looking for employment. Mr. Honeycutt, owner of the food barn, had just built a beautiful formal dining facility adjacent to the food barn. He placed an advertisement looking for an experienced restaurant manager that could make his facility a premier dining spot. Terri Hartly found out that there was an opening for this job. It was a very fine day in may when Terri entered the office of Mr. Honeycutt to be interviewed. She presented her resume and showed great excitement in taking on the immense responsibility. She explained to Mr. Honeycutt that she wanted to name the facility Terri's food barn restaurant. She said, "when you put your meat on sale on the second and third days, i will buy that fresh product. If will buy the beef, pork, chicken, seafood, and produce and present them as absolutely fresh meat and present it on a beautiful menu. I want our customers to know that we only serve fresh, not frozen, meat. This will be our motto in our byline that i will advertise in our local papers. I will hire butchers and bakers from your food barn to work a second shift, if they wish, which will commence at four in the afternoon every day. They might, with their experience and recipes, even enjoy cooking. You will see a menu that will top many of the famous restaurants you have heard about. Because, if i get this job there is a known chef from the food service college that will relocate to assist me in this grand endeavor."

Terri continued, "The hours will be from four to eight o'clock p.m. And eventually will be limited to reservation only. I will hire and train folks from our town to be waiters and waitresses. The plan will be to market one of the most choice and best restaurants in the state not only for food, but in special service and friendliness." Terri asked if she could name the restaurant Terri's food barn restaurant.

I'll tell you now that there was a suggestion of a romantic relationship between a trained European chef, Mr. Ralph cutler, and Terri. He would give these American meat delights a new twist and a new presentation besides cooking the standard every day meat recipes. Mr. Cutler was just plain as could be. He wore blue jeans and a plaid shirt when he wasn't working at their restaurant.

As a lad he would work as a rancher in Texas and speak with a Texas twang. To be clear, he was an apprentice to two European chefs over a two-year period. One of the chefs was French and the other was Italian. From them he acquired some great culinary skills.

Mr. Honeycutt read the resume and heard Terri's plan. He said in two words, "you're hired! I will pay you ten percent of the profits if you do. Your income will exceed your expectations -- even mine!"

Since the opening a year Ago i, William Worthy, have eaten there many times and I promise you it was great food and a great experience with outstanding service. Now, a year later, I will want and can go there. You will indeed have to have reservations. Our town can revel in the knowledge that we have another great successful business in our town port haven refuge.

Ice Cream Parlor

Ms. Coney was pleasurably and pleasingly plump. It was commonly known that she was eating more ice cream than she was selling. It didn't help that the ice cream was settling in her derriere. It was a case where her tastey cone business was more of a break-even affair than one for profit.

Ms. Coney started making her own ice cream and her profits soared. She got the recipe from her grandma's ice cream churning. Happy eating!!

Port Haven's Library

Ms. Merriam was a librarian and honored graduate in literature from Harvard. Our library was soon to be blessed by a huge collection of literature containing a multitude of subjects. I cannot think of a subject that was not covered by the volmes of literature which our library was about to receive.

This massive book collection was given to port haven refuge by a philanthropist. Her name was Mallory Herschfield. Her name will be displayed above the entrance. She had recently passed away and was one of grandfather worthy's best friends.

What a tremendous boon to our city. Our librarian graduated with honors in literature and teaching. Her only habit was chewing and popping gum during quiet time at the library. The books came with card indexes to help organize the books. The key note to a great town is having a great library - thanks to grandfather worthy.

Our Town Barber Shop

To go there, or even looking in the window as you passed by, was a unique experience. Some folks will go out of their way to see the tallest barber they may ever see, by the name of ray shears. His seven foot frame sprouted a black curly head of hair and handlebar moustache stationed just below a hawk shaped, wonderously large nose. Above that admirable nose were two smiling magenta blue eyes, shielded by long eyelashes. When he looked at you, you knew you had been looked at by friendly eyes. Mounted above those brillant eyes were bushy, black eyebrows. A mass of sideburns extended to his jaw bone. His hair wasn't long. It was just to his barbar shop jacket collar. Resting below that great moustache were his full lips. He must have been born with that perpetual smile. Those lips topped a large square chin, with an iprint that some people would call a dimple.

He was one of those men that never seemed to grow old. He looked like he was thirty years old. His large chin led to a muscled, somewhat wrinkled, throat that led to a pair of shoulders that were like a pro-football lineman. Adjacent to his wide shoulders was a massive chest. Hanging from his shoulders were large arms with bulging biceps. From his elbows to his hands he was more slender. His hands and his fingers were strong. This was to be expected because there was a long line of customers in his chair from opening to close.

Mr. Shears was spotlessly clean. His barber jacket hung to his knees and was always as white as snow. His pants were black and let to black shiny shoes. This, besides the fact that he once taught in a barber school, helped him to be admired in his shop. He used his barbaring talents in Hollywood. Ray met a beautiful woman named Lisa. She was a real "dreamboat". She now has a little desk in the shop where she takes appointments and has a list of gentlement that ask her to manicure their nails. She went out to Hollywood to become an actress and found herself in a barbershop doing manicures to get by. It was there that she met ray shears. He dated this lovely girl and within months they married in Hollywood. She talked ray into coming to her home town, port haven refuge.

Normally kids hate to get their hair cut, but now in ray's shop, when they climb aboard ray's hydrolic chair, he would pump up his chair to full height and tell them little stories as he would cut their hair. The ride upwards in that chair was fun to the kids and i think some men enjoyed this ride too! The children would ask ray to show them his sharp straight razor and show them how he sharpened the razor. Ray did the sharpening of the blade on a leather strop which hung on the side of his barbar chair. The boys always knew that there would be a chunk of hard candy that ray would give them as he brougth them back down to earth in his hydrolic chair.

Because ray worked in Hollywood he was able to give a man any style of hair cut they desired. Men left the barber shop with haircuts that they never thought they would wear. Many of the men were told by their wives that they looked more handsome and glamorous with their new Hollywood haircut.

The women of the town insisted there be a ladies day only, where they would be provided some exotic hair styles that were in vogue and current styles in Hollywood. An appointment was needed as he was booked two months ahead. His wife Lisa was reluctant to have her husband practice his art on the ladies. She attempted to screen appointments and ride to select middle-aged and older ladies for their hair appointments.

Ray and his glamorous wife attented sunday school at reverand Wiseley's church without fail every sunday. There is no question that the congregation increased just to be near and been seen around the handsoe couple and have casual conversation with them. Did I tell you that ray could play the accordian and his wife could sing? They were a hit at church picnics. Ray cam to know our new town better than Hollywood.

P.s. Ray, before barber school, was a professional wrestler which accounted partly for his strength and appearance. He learned the accorddian from his immigrant father. I could not tell you what his nationality was. It was a mystery to everyone. We found out that his descendants were bulgarian. We jokingly referred to him as the "Mucle bulging Bulgarian". It was okay with ray and Lisa loved it.

His apparrel, away from the barbershop with his wife, consisted of bright white suits and bright ties. This, together with his seven foot frame, never failed to catch the eye of everyone and their pets that were on leashes or loose. Lisa was probably more alluring than many of our old-fashioned citizens would approve. These were the clothes she bought in Hollywood boutiques. Success abounds for ray and Lisa shears.

Taxi

I must not forget that we have a Chinaman, named Foo Chu, living in our town. I'm sure he is an immigrant, because he mostly uses hand signals to get his message across.

He arrived in our town on a river barge that docked at our port. I was told he was working as a deckhand. I guess he skipped ship! He must have brought with him some valuables for he was paid by the ship captain in American money.

Amazingly, he had enough cash to buy a car. He had it painted bright red, with the words taxi on both sides. On the trunk and the hood, he had "taxi" printed in Chinese. It is our only taxi and he is never without a rider.

His problem was that he didn't know the value of an American dollar. He unfortunately was charging riders less than the value of the taxi's cost for gas. Sherrif Gunderson told Mr. Foo Chu that he would have to get a license for the taxi and well as a business license.

Gunderson's deputy, Virgil Cain, took him to those agencies that helped him fill out the forms and pay the fees. It almost took foo Chu's last dollar to pay this and be legal.

Our kind deputy then told him what a normal charge for a taxi ride should be for within the town's limits and another price for the out-of-town costs.

Mr. Chu found he had a bountiful profit as a taxi man. He seemed not to ever lack for riders and was making money.

He lived at the port in a small room that Thelma's fishery owned and was made available.

Problem: he said he was seeking a companion and asked where he would find a nice Chinese lady he might marry from the town. He was then made aware that he was the only Chinese person living in port haven reguge. So foo started seeking out other ladies that had been available for a few years, who had not found a mate for one reason or another. His eventual success and willingness to stay here may have been put in jeopardy. The only other person in the town that could speak Mandarin Chinese was the librarian. He spent a lot of time at the library as a result. The librarian and foo began a lasting relationship.

To you I say "Good luck Foo Chu"!

Cosmetologist

A recent graduate of a cosmetologist school in Chicago, who graduated with honors, could not find a place to practice her skills because there were too many other beauty salons. Carolyn combs, who was also a graduate of our town, thought that port haven refuge might be a great place to practice her art.

She went to a good high school friend named dolly who insisted that she come to our town. Carolyn would live in dolly's home until she was established in business.

Carolyn combs, with her father's support came to port haven refuge and rented one of the few locations remaining on main street. Carolyn's first investment was to have a neon sign made and erected in front of the building space and above the door where she would make her name known. The sign said "Carolyn's curls". Her dad financed the furniture and the chair from which Carolyn would practice her trade.

Carolyn would provide the most recent hairstyles to the young ladies of the town. The young ladies in their teens and twenties, flocked to her salon to receive her exciting presentations of hair styles for the young at heart.

Succeed she did! It was not just her find work at being a cosmetologist, but because she had a wonderful personality and listened to the women as they explained their plights in life.

Listening well and remembering names will always be the key to being liked and even loved and she was adept at both remembering and listening.

The Electric Company

I have met Mr. Elmo Voltly and found him to have an electric personality. Ha! Ha! You would notice that his crew cut stood three or four inches high and stood straight up. If guessed that Elmo had received too many jolts of volts when he was a lineman. Elmo employed two "grunts" to add or replace poles and string electric line. He hired another employee to install and maintain meters for businesses. Wlmo put two meter readers on staff.

It seemed all of his employees took too much time off. When the billing lady, sally forth, was AWOL and bills were not sent to receive revenue, payday would be late. Sally forth had to be sent packing.

Elmo was afraid to fire her. Sally had a mean streak with a bad temper as well. Mr. Forth, sally's husband, had a police record. Poor Elmo, I wondered what he would do. Elmo's staff was threatening to quit because of the postponement of pay. Elmo fired sally and word was out that Mr. Forth would give him a thrashing and his new car would get a beating as well. Elmo would meet fire with fire.

Elmo's wife's name was bertha. She was a muscular, Russian woman. She went to the home of sally forth and said, "if your husband even touches Elmo you will be heading to the E.R."

Elmo advertised to fill the billing job. After a number of interviews, Elmo found the perfect person for the job. A graduate from business college that had a great smile and a soft pleasant voice. Her voice would be great for phone calls. She was well dressed and well groomed in every way and she knew exactly what billing was all about.

She knew what to say when customers were delinquent in paying. Her name was Carla Lincoln-Jefferson. And, oh yes, she was the first African-American lady I had ever hired in our town. On wow, did the work spread! This was just the year when the African-American folks were getting a "place" in a white society. Carla was twenty-something and had a husband who was mostly away on a boxing circuit. His wages were varied depending on his wins and losses. As yet, Carla is without child.

I encouraged the business lads to make her feel welcome and to follow the J.C. Penney rule – it was "do unto others as you would have them do unto you". Carla promptly got the revenue flowing and the employees paid. Carla was certainly good under fire and this was especially noted when a storm caused a power outage. Carla now acted as Elmos' secretary. She knew and could do the job. She would call in the fire department, tree trimmer and all the members of the staff when there was the trauma of power outages.

Wouldn't you know it! Bertha now worked as a purchasing agent for the electric company. Believe me, with her demeanor and stature, there would not be many salesmen or companies that would argue with her over contracts and prices. I told bertha this was nepotism by hiring ones family. Bertha then remembered that Mr. Innman, the innkeeper, was working his family. I said to her that this was no argument ove pay. It had something to do with a little power. I thought to myself that if Carla became ill what would the company do? So Carla asked Elmo "would you please hire an apprentice for me?"

Elmo said that he thought this might be a problem with sally. He avoided interviewing and hired Carla's sister Bessie. Her sister graduated from business school as well. Carla could get the billing and collections out earlier.

For Elmo and his wife bertha, life was much better – all be because of Carla Lincoln-Jefferson and her sister. However, Bessie was appropriating cash payments that were to the electric company into her own pocket. Woe is me! When her sister Carla found about this, Bessie was no longer a citizen of the town.

Postal Department

It was decided that port haven refuge was to have a post office. So, they had one built by the edge of town. Getting the mail from the drug store would no longer happen. It was anticipated that eventually, as the town grew, the post office would be ready for an abundance of mailings. I am happy to report that this year the post office was completed.

it was already said that the government spent too much money on it. We should not have built such a massive structure. The sign above the entrance read: "the united states of America post office". These were the times that the government became acutely aware that there should be quotas set for hiring of blacks and whites and other nationalities. So, it was no surprise that a middle-aged well-educated high school graduate was given the job as post master of the post office. His name was Robert Townsend.

The office, as i am speaking, has just opened and i see the residents marching up to the entrance while all the town was taking in the beauty of the new post office.

That day many of the residents would be purchasing post office boxes, posting mail, and buying stamps. There were two postal employees providing services. There was one mail truck that would be bringing in mail every day. The mail would be sorted by two workers in the mail room. By the way, the sorters were African-American and were named Joshua and Jeremiah. They were brothers. They were hired by the post office general after meeting security requirements. They were told there would be no delivery to the townspeople's home at this point.

Revenue would not permit the hiring of truck drivers and mailmen to deliver to homes and businesses in this relatively small town. They promised that ultimately when the town grew and revenue increased there would be delivery services to homes.

This was a time that discrimination was at its highest. No one wanted to be a neighbor of an African-American. What now?

The post master wrote a letter to all of the businesses of port haven refuge with a government stamp. He stated: first think of the name of your community, second remember and please accept them as American citizens too! Who will step up and find a place for our African-American friends to live? Even i, will worthy, would think there would be some need for low-income housing and apartments. Several of the apartments were still unoccupied. The new African-Americans who were residents promptly rented them.

Port Haven Refuge Law Firm

After the will was signed leaving me the port haven's refuge, I was visited by a legal team and a major real estate broker. They said grandpa had agreed to sell port haven estate. They had every intention of proving it. They said that all I had to do was sign the papers and I would be a wealthy man. I told them to get the hell off the property. I know that grandpa would never have said those things. They left in a hurry and said, "We will be back and you will lose your case!" It still is a worry to me as to when this might happen. They have not come back as yet. God, I hoped not!

Now i have to contend with the state governor's office and association, for they had decided that port haven refuge was a grand place, and large enough to be made into a state park. If necessary they would take it under the guise of public domain. I said to myself, "now what will i do?" I asked that the college president of law studies and teaching refer me to his best senior graduate for i now needed an attorney.

I contacted the attorney he recommended. I was assigned Justin law to fight the state from usurping the port haven refuge properties and estates. Though, eventually, Justin went to court and proved that not only was the sanctuary part of the estate but so were six of the town's businesses which sat on the estate property. My grandpa willed the six businesses these properties. The will stated that these businesses could use the portion of the estate on which their businesses were located. The state would have to include these businesses as part of the public domain. At that time the six businesses presented couner lawsuits against the state for attempting to put them out of business. The state would have to pay them one million dollars if they pursued with their order of public domain. All of the other town busineses and local farmers wrote to the governor and the state officials and said, "We will see to it that you get voted out of office!"

What is really funny is that all of this mess could have been avoided. The simple truth is that this property would not ever fall under public domain because it was purchased from the government in 1776. Today they call this a "grandfather" clause. It was part of the free land offer for those moving west. The federal government had priority over the state rules!

The Court House

The city acquired a proper building space to be our new court house. A judge moved to our town to take charge of this important position. His name was ben courtly.

Judge courtly would apply justice. Wiley Gunderson would send petty thieves – speeders, domestic disputes, druns, bar fighters, and all other law-breakers that you could think of to Courtly's court for payment of fines or incarceration.

It seems like nepotism permeated our town because the judge hired his wife to be his typist and clerk. All fines were collected by Mrs. Courtly. All fines received were turned over to the city revenue department, which I might add, was in sore need of cash to operate the city. All business owners would receive property tax forms and would pay on them according to the values of the land and property. With these funds they could pay the animal shelters and veterinarian who applied their skills there.

In the very same building, we had a licence bureau which was run by Mr. Taggert. His job was to issue licences for dogs and cats as well as fishing and hunting permits!

Since this was a state job it included the licencing of all types of vehicles. These funds along with the others were sent to the state bank. The funds collected were for the animal shelter and veterinarian.

Mr. Dreadsome, who worked in licencing, required driving tests for everyone. Driving tests were given by tom speeder. He could give a driving test while sleeping with his eyes open! This is the reason that no one failed the driving test. To my knowledge i think a blind man could have passed the test.

Assessment Department

The assessment department is located in the court house building.

We loved to call her sally the assessor. She was the department head. She would have a so-called expert evaluate our property. It was a wonder to everyone as to how this bumbling fool could say what our property was worth and assign an asset value. Each year everyone had to shell out their hard-earned money to pay the state.

If you argued about it, that numbskull would add value to our property and charge us more. You cannot beat those state bureaucrats.

Oh, i know very well that we all hate to pay our taxes but feel better in knowing that the funds would support the mental health department, the library, the park, and most of the schools' needs, as well as the animal shelters, etc.

I, will worthy, have many protests as to how she equated the cost of property in pursuing reconciliation to the state and proof of how she made her decision on evaluations. I won't be giving in.

P.S. Sally was an especially good friend of her boss the governor.

The License Bureau

The state agency manager of the license bureau would change with the election of every new governor as did the manager of all state agencies.

Melody, the current manager of this agency and her associate would test applicants for licenses; occasionally, written and eye tests were given. Sometimes the actual driving test would be administered by another assistant of the team, or the entire team. The administer of the test was said to snooze with his eyes open during a test. Its no wonder everyone passed.

Melody would collect taxes and licences from all new buyers of vehicles of any sort. She also collected fees for fishing licences and dog licences. The animal shelter was also under her area of responsibility.

Melody was a beautiful elderly lady. She was very stern when dealing with customers – no smiles. I found this to be true of the employees in most government agencies. I would wonder if it was the nature of the work or was it because their term as manager was short-lived as the office of the governor. Most of us thought that her name should have been "moody" instead of melody.

How she established all the fees must be a trade secret. And I have a legitimate claim against the state on this matter.

Marriage License Bureau

The last, but most memorable, office in the court house was the marriage license bureau. I had one occasion to go there when I married Jeannette. The appointment was just long enough to meet the license lady.

We completed the necessary forms and l when we received the results we were granted permission to marry. It was just a license, only it was the addest moment when we discovered that the lady behind the counter was a spinster. We both wondered if she received a strange fulfillment in handling the paper work from the love birds seeking a license.

The Fire Department

On any day, except for inclimate weather, you could see our fire department men cleaning and shining the fire truck and equipment. The fire chief, Smokey Waterson, would have it no other way. After all, the tax payers, along with joseph worthy had purchased the largest and most modern fire truck in the state. It was enjoyable just to drive by and look at it and wave at the firemen. God, how our kids loved to get out of their car and go meet the men in the fire department. They would let the boys get behind the wheel of the truck and hit the siren. It got so folks didn't know whether it was a real fire or the little boys blowing the truck sirens. Have you ever known young boys that did not want a toy fire truck for Christmas?

Fire service was still available twenty-four hours a day. There were three men on each shift. They ate and slept there on the second floor. They cooked their own meals and no smoking. No girlfriends were allowed to visit. Smokey's men could read, or watch T.V., otherwise they would clean the station or truck, or would be on a fire call. They not only handled fires but auto wrecks and traumas at residences.

Most of Smokey's calls were to put out grass fires or to go to a car wreck in their area or on the highways. There would also be an ambulance from a small but effective hospital. The firemen were very excited on their fire calls. They also installed smoke alarms and electric fans for indigent folks on hot summer days.

Smokey was an ex-cowboy from the west and moved to our town. It follows that on excepting the fire chief job, he still wore his cowboy hat. He continued to fancy himself as a hero of the old west. He had managed several ranches at some distance in another state. He worked in several states as a ranch hand. He chewed tobacco. He was six feet six inches tall. He had a ruddy complexion. He wore cowboy boots and cowboy belt. He was proud to show his belt buckle which was given to him after winning a bull riding event: but he donned that fire chief hat and clothes whenever there was an incident. He even insisted on driving the truck. He drove the fire truck as if he were riding a stallion.

P.S. Every noon he would cut loose with a firehouse siren for fifteen seconds. He let everyone know he was on duty and ready to serve – which he did!

The Hospital

Yes, even great grandpa worthy had given financial assistance in starting up our private hospital in port haven refuge. When i was a kid i had my tonsils taken out there. The hospital had many large windows. It had a granite exterior. It was built to last forever. A sister named Francis was the senior director of the entire hospital. She had her organizational chart like the Militarys' and had a chief nurse for each segment of the hospitals' departments.

The departments included were: the emergency rooms, admissions, patient rooms, janitorial services, food service, surgery, x-rays and radiation, billing department and the doctors' offices. The hospital also had a chapel.

Our patient care was set up where each nurse was accountable for seven patients. Assignments were made every day. A head nurse named robin, with flaming red hair which matched her personality, would let you know if you got out of line or didn't do your job. You had better know that you had been talked to.

You would think that such a large hospital was too big for our community. You should know that there were three smaller towns whose doctors sent patients to his hospital for care. Of course, the doctors would treat the patients who were sent there. They would be seen by a doctor who specialized in that patients' specific problem.

I can't remember the names of all the professionals and workers because there were so many that worked with the hospital.

I know all this because I had an occasion to be admitted for treatment and care.

The hospital diagnostic equipment was the best available. This was because some of our more affluent residents had given donations or bequeathed considerable offerings to that end. The hospital decided where to apply the offerings and they applied them to the equipment and mechanical beds. I pray that my readers have no opportunity to experience the care and activities of the hospital, except for, of course, injury or illness. Thank god for the emergency room!

We have a medical practioner that had looked everywhere to find a place where he could practice his medicine. And finally settled on our town. He is now in his sixties. Dr. Ted Mendmen had been schooled in several places in an attempt to get a medical license. Some wonder if he bought the thing. Nevertheless, the license stated that he was now a doctor and had the authority to practice medicine.

Dr. Mendmen attended school and received a dental license before he went to medical college. Dr. Mendmen mentioned to his patients about his dental license which hung on the wall and said "I would like to see your teeth and check on your need for dental care. Consider this a bonus for there will not be a charge." Some patients even asked, "can you do the work?" The doctor replied, "I would love to, but I am just doing this as a favor to my patients. If will give you a consultation and diagnosis for your medical problems."

He had a one room office on main street, where his wife would assist with the phone and collect payments. We found that Ted Mendmen worked the boxing circuit for some time and was skilled in lacerations and abrasions and all the other injuries a body could endure.

Our doctor was friendly and talked to all of his patients. It was the older townspeopole that sought him out for his remedies. Indeed, our Dr. Ted Mendmen had an abundance of them, some of which were thought to have been conjured up by the doctor himself.

His patients would find a cure coming on as the doctor tried his snake oil. He was careful. I know for a fact he had procured an abundance of the "old western town" medicine called Lauden. That was all the westerners knew of at that time, including his older patients. Frankly, it was a narcotic laced with alcohol.

In another era a doctor was considered a gatekeeper. Therefore, Dr. Mendmen would send his patients to the E.R. Or hospital for any anything serious. But cure he did, the many household ailments from sore throats to headaches. The doctor did not treat younger folks. They did not seek ted out for doctoring. The joke around town was that they wished he would stop "practicing" and cure more severe ailments.

There is a secret here. Our doctor had received training at the mayo clinic. The secret is that the doctor had training and knowledge to treat more serious ailments and diseases, but he was reluctant to take on such heavy responsibilities. He didn't have the courage to practice his art. However, don't get me wrong, I liked him and so did everyone else, except for the medical staff at the general hospital.

Tourist Information

For those planning to stop here on your vacation, I know you would want to hear what to expect on your tour. As of now you have read most of the details about the origin of this sanctuary. I will now give a quick description of the refuge.

You will find three-hundred acres of plush green areas consisting of paths and ponds. Name a tree and you will find it on this retreat. We have seven ponds. The ponds are deep and spring fed. There is one large lake that is also spring fed. The larger ponds are to the north. Most of the geese seem to prefer these larger ponds. The ducks have a preference for the smaller ponds but they still frequent the larger ponds as well. The geese will also visit the smaller ponds. You know from earlier in the narrative that the ponds are full of "small-fry" fish provided by Thelma, with whom I had a deal. In all, there are five miles of shoreline. The geese prefer the northern area where there is less activity. They would follow the tree line when they flew from place to place.

The entire refuge is surrounded by wooden fencing – obviously no wires. The refuge area and entrance, paths and booths are only a part of this grand estate.

Our Newspaper: The Sentinel

I am proud to say that our local newspaper, called the sentinel, always looked to me, William Worthy, to present all the information I have and the stories of the townspeople and businesses. Mainly because I know them, love them, and want to tell their stories. Believe me, it took little to present an abundance of news to the sentinel. I might add, the sentinel does have other news—marriages, births, anniversaries and advertisements from all of our local businesses and national news as well.

The editor of the sentinel is chuck copy. He would put anything in the sentinel including all the gossip he could get just to make the paper more interesting. The gossip always started with "I heard that…." Or "it was told to me….". On my, how the readers loved gossip. As advertising revenue kept increasing, the plan was to add at least one more advertising sales person and two reporters.

It is evident, week by week, that plan of chuck copy's was coming true!

Wentsworth College Prep and Highschool

Mrs. Booker was principal of our school which turned out scholars who were heading off to college. The dean of the college, Mr. Proctor, was renowned for the geniuses that were born from his eloquent speaking and teaching knowledge.

The trade school students were those that wished to become skilled in a craft before applying for apprenticeship under the many contractors and builders of our fine growing city. These student apprentices and workmen were looking to get an income as soon as possible.

The junior and senior proms were both exciting and sad. Some good friends, in going their own ways, would probably not see each other again. Others, including the cut-ups, would not now worry about being expelled for their heavy drinking and trying what they call "Mary jane", or dumping loads of vodka, or other booze, in the punch.

Techar Totter, I must not forget her name or her class, was known for being one of the premier drama teachers in the state. She was a renowned actress in her own right. Many of her students were eventually seen in movies and on T.V.

"bully" tamer was a star actor in all the senior plays. Tilly was glamorous and had a body the other girls yearned for. She was the leading lady in those junior and senior plays. There were many other excellent supporting actors. I am sure all of them would find themselves in T.V. And movie roles one day.

Mrs. Phroggsbottom who had an accute desire to teach science and biology and decided to.

The graduates for the next year or two would be proclaiming "thoses were the days my friend, I thought they would never end." Wentsworth high school was and still is unique. Can you recall seeing the movie "grease"? Who hasn't? Well if you have you'd be seeing a high school much like ours. Wentsworth, like all high schools, has its sports hero. There is always that quarterback who, with his entourage, would stroll the halls showing off his letter jacket or sweater. He didn't have to look back to know girls were watching him and wished they could date him. This years' hero was josh. His special hangout along with his wannabe or wish I weres was the town drug store. You see, we have one of the oldest soda fountains that can be found in any drug store in the U.S.

There josh would go to the soda bar where his cronies would buy him his favorite ice cream called tutti-frutti. The store even had a small dance floor just like in the good ole days. Girls and boys liked to show off the latest dance to the latest music. They all thought they had the skills of terpsichory.

In those days the guys or young men that hung out there were called drug store cowboys, and the guys making the sodas were called soda jerks. Today you can find many of these high school sports heroes performing simple hum-drum jobs throughout the town.

I am just old enough to remember the old times and young enough to experience the new times. I'd say I'm caught in the middle, which allows me the privilege of talking about the folks that live and love in our town. We can boast that we have one of the few remaining drive-in theaters. It is still the number one place where guys take their dates. Good thing too, our old theater still runs old movies. The owner of the old palace theater is still showing old movies. There's an interest by the new generation to see those movies that their folks talked about. Between the old movie equipment and the old film there are still burn-outs where the movie goes dark and the operator has to splice the film. The kids still yell and jeer whenever that happens but for some couples it's a great time to steal a kiss or two!

Entertainment in our town includes the movies and drive-ins, bbqs, visiting friends, entertaining relatives, holiday get-togethers, church events. The ladies use to dress up in their finery for all events, but now it's limited to church, interviewing for jobs, weddings and funerals. It's interesting to note that currently no one dresses up for anything except for a fancy restaurant and interviews or funerals.

Those young boys that were too young for most jobs have found that babysitting, dog walking, yard work and snow removal would earn enough for basic necessities such as candy and games. There are several young enterprising entrepreneurs that have found they can earn some serious money by selling night crawlers which takes no small effort to find and keep alive. They get ten cents a worm which they sell to many fishermen.

The Nook

I mentioned earlier I this story that I had not yet met the woman I could live my life with. Well I think it may have happened. You see, every morning I would drive my little scooter up to "the nook breakfast café". I would go in and sit alone in a booth. I thought it was more comfortable there. Every day, the nook's owner, Jeannette, would bring me coffee. It was hot and steamy. She would say with a smile, "good morning William, I hope you have a wonderful day!" I would heave a sigh and study the entirty of her, and think I'd like to date her someday.

The very next day when she brought my morning brew I said, "will you go out to dinner with me?" I was thinking maybe the pizza place. Jeannette responded, "how about we have dinner right here? You know my house is attached to the breakfast nook. I'll fix something I know that you would like, and we'll watch T.V." And I said, "and hold hands?"

There was so much detail I could explain after the many dates I had with her most of which were remarkable and will remain very private and bound forever in my heart. The best date we had was when we walked the paths of our bird refuge. While strolling through the sanctuary I asked Jeannette if she knew the song "getting to know you?". She said "yes I do". I said "can you sing it?" She said, "I certainly can." I said "will you?" She said "okay" and gave me a moment or two. Then the sweetest words I ever heard came out of her mouth. "getting to know you, getting to know all about you……" when she was through I thanked her so much. That was the sweetest moment of our relationship.

Of the eight benches in the park, I love them all. I think we must have sat on all of them. We were as the old folks say, "sparking" and telling all about our past. It was a starry night and the moon shone brightly. We sat down by a garden wall and said nothing. We just held hands. Sometimes words just get in the way and are a nuisance. On this date I got my first kiss from Jeannette.

Jeannette graduated from heaven's portal high school with honors. She said, "until now I've had no feelings for any man in particular". I said to her on that eighth bench, "would you marry me?". She was startled. She said, "thank you, I will and I do". I said "we are going to have a splendid wedding. She said "when?" I said "this moment Jeannette."

I'll tell you now my readers to imagine the most lavish. Splendid wedding you have ever known. That is exactly what I gave Jeannette. Her dad gave her away that day. Mr. Lacer, her dad, happened to own a farm. We talked a lot about that wonderful day. We live in the manor now. Tessie takes care of the both of us as though we were her children. I am one happy man.

If there is any sorrow in port haven refuge it is when the town grew and the element of crime and drugs creeped into the essence of their city. Our problem in growth is that the federal, state, and county all want to tax everything and everybody. In our little port haven refuge, which is in it's embryonic stage, there were political and government agencies that tried to usurp the few dollars of the few that earned. This is a heartfelt thought that i am reluctant to put into words about a town that is full of successful and happy people.

The other factor is just like in your city that the drug and crime rates are increasing and at this point in time no one knows how to stop it. It is way over the sheriffs and deputy's abilities to cope with this kind of menace.

Our sheriff, Mr. Gunderson, has asked if port haven refuge could have at least two federal agents trained in these problems - to set up an office and start dealing with these horrendous problems. Just recently there was a letter sent to the mayor that a request for an FBI service agency to hire people who would be assigned to our town's problems. God, I hope so.

CONCLUSION

It has been fun relating to you what I know about my family-Joseph and Joe Worthy- the founders of port haven refuge and the port on the river. There are many more events of the past, but believe me, this should be enough for now.

Jeannette and I are raising our son who we call "sky" worthy. It seems, by his current growth, he will be a tall man, topped by a dark reddish blond crop of hair. He will be raised in the manor.

There is a plan that he will soon have a sister to play and argue with on the grounds. Tessie is not going to be with much longer. She and her husband have two children also and they are being taught to carry on with the duties that she and her husband have provided all these years for the manor. We are going to have quite a family, white and dark, living in this manor. "Sky" and our daughter will be taught to share the worthy income of our town in helping to supply the needs of the refuge sanctuary and town emergencies if there are any.

In effect, this is a narrative that will not end, as the worthy generations will continue. Jeannette and i thank you for reading this narrative of the worthy family. Now I must put this story to bed.

Signed: William and Jeannette Worthy

PORT HAVEN

I PAINTED THIS SCENE AS I SAW IT AT ONE OF THE SANCTUARY PONDS.
IT WAS IN MEMORY OF THE LIVES OF GRANDFATHER JOE WORTHY AND HIS
DAD JOSEPH.

Printed in the United States
By Bookmasters